SANJAY

SHULI ZHAO

Made with ❤ on the Notion Press Platform
www.notionpress.com

Contents

Introduction

Sanjay was notorious in the village for his bad habits. The first one was pilfering. When he visited a fellow villager, the house owner would stare at Sanjay until he left. When he passed farmland, people who were ploughing the land should look after their clothes and tobacco pipe in case of being stolen. Anyone in the village who lost domestic animals or something would firstly visit Sanjay's home and check whether Sanjay was at home or not. However, Sanjay was an important figure when someone died---preparing graveclothes, carrying the coffin and digging the grave couldn't be done without him.

Sanjay was also proficient in cultivating lands, and he could do the work of two. Even so, no one would like to hire him because Sanjay would gamble even if he only had twenty cents. People whose terrace edge subsided were willing to pay double to Sanjay since the weir that he mended was solid. However, employers must supervise him in case of losing something. Later, Sanjay served as a bugler[1] for which his elder family member Vasin wanted to bury him alive[2], so he ran away and didn't come back until the National Revolutionary Army liberated the village after the end of World War II[3]. Seeing Sanjay's poor situation, the village cadre wanted to help him but was told that Sanjay was a bad guy. After most righteous people who were misunderstood as undesirable elements were redressed, the story of Sanjay was known by village cadres.

[1] Buglers often act in funerals, weddings and other activities.

[2] At that time, working as a bugler was regarded as disgraceful and shameful for the whole family.

[3] Here refers to Japanese aggression in China during World War II.

CHAPTER ONE

When Sanjay was 12 years old, his father died. His mother fed the family by weaving cloth. Sanjay was a hard-working and smart boy who could weed and plow seed at the age of twelve. He could also do the chores like an adult when he was around 16 years old but he was less capable in carrying a load. It was at that time when his mother arranged him a nine-year-old child bride[1] --- Damayanti who also came from a poor family. Her parents died and her brother couldn't feed her, so she was sent to Sanjay's family.

Sanjay's mother treated Damayanti fairly[2] --- the wise woman who only had a son, so she treated her daughter-in-law as her own children. Sanjay joined the village self-entertainment group[3] in which he learned opera. Sanjay was a remarkable performer in the group since he was a boy. In the second year she came to the village, Damayanti went to watch the play performed by self-entertainment group. Other children would joke that "It's your husband, Damayanti!" when Sanjay came out, which embarrassed Damayanti. Gradually, people were accustomed to it and no longer teased her. In terms of watching the play, at first, Damayanti only enjoyed the lively atmosphere but later she found that her husband was very handsome compared with other actors. Therefore, she would go to watch the opera even though she was busy. After watching Sanjay's performance, she would come back home in case of being reprimanded by mother.

There was a time when Sanjay played to the end, so Damayanti was late for preparing dinner and was scolded. She just broke into snigger. Sanjay knew the reasons so he also smiled and said "Why not come back earlier" instead of blaming her.

[1] It refers to a young girl who is adopted and grows up to be a daughter-in-law.

[2] At that time, daughter-in-law were mostly treated harshly.

[3] It is a folk organization in which members will sing, dance and play opera.

CHAPTER TWO

When Sanjay was 23 years old, his mother was sick, vomiting all she ate. She knew she couldn't survive the disease, and their neighbor auntie also advised Sanjay to prepare the funeral. Sanjay's mother saw the doctor at Vasin's medicine shop many times but she didn't recover despite taking many medicines.

One day, Sanjay's mother told the neighbor auntie: "I know I couldn't survive the winter." "Don't think negatively." The neighbor auntie interrupted "No one is immune from disease." Sanjay's mother said: "I know myself best. I am not afraid of death. However, there is only one thing that concerns me---Sanjay and Damayanti. Damayanti is 15 years old so it's time to hold the wedding. There are few members in my family so I hope you can help us in the process." Hearing this, the neighbor auntie asked for wedding date and promised to help.

Their wedding was held on 26th July. Damayanti's brother also participated in the wedding. Vasin, as the elder family member, entertained guests at tangwu room[1] Sanjay's mother cooked chicken instead of tofu on the special day.

The wedding finally ended. Sanjay's mother was satisfied with the sound relationship between Sanjay and Damayanti since they knew each other for a long time.

However, Sanjay's mother was on the verge of death with the decreasing temperature after harvest---she even put on cotton-padded jacket in September but still felt cold. Same as before, Sanjay's mother had stomach ache and vomited all she ate. She had livid rings round her eye and she was so skinny that her cheekbones were prominent.

Sanjay was told by the neighbor auntie again that "I'm afraid that your mother couldn't make it through. You'd better prepare the funeral." Actually, Sanjay knew the situation clearly so he went to seek help from Vasin.

Vasin whose medicine shop sold medicine and sundry supplies like coffins made of polar, said: "We have all things ready." However, Vasin had a rule that people must write an IOU to him no matter what they used. He told his children that lending money for interest made more profits than doing business.

Sanjay's mother died after autumn harvest. Damayanti, as a teenager with less life experience, only cried. Twenty-three-year-old Sanjay was only a little better than her. He was busy preparing the funeral---finding people to carry the coffin and practice geomancy---so he had no time left for his own family. Fortunately, the neighbor auntie helped Damayanti make mourning cap, hang white shoes, cook noodles[2], thus finishing the funeral.

Sanjay owed Vasin thirty yuan[3] (including both principal and interest) for cloth, household supplies and coffin for preparing the wedding and funeral, and Sanjay wrote an IOU.

[1] The main (south-facing) room of a Chinese house

[2] These are essential parts of traditional Chinese funeral.

[3] One yuan equals to a hundred cents.

CHAPTER THREE

Sanjay and Damayanti totally had 4 mu[1] farmland. They were concerned that they couldn't return money to Vasin so they worked as long-term farm laborer[2] for him. Damayanti started to learn about weaving when she was not high enough to touch the weaving machine. Therefore, she was proficient at weaving at 16 years old. Every day, the young couple woke up early and did their own jobs to pay back debts.

Vasin employed four laborers to plow the land. The veteran praised Sanjay a smart and capable man. Although he was too old to do physically strenuous activities, the veteran was Sanjay's knowledgeable teacher.

Sanjay ran out of grains for the wedding and funeral last year, so he kept lending grains until harvest this year. In October, Vasin gave Sanjay pay according to the food price in spring. Although he paid off 30 yuan debts, Sanjay still had to pay 10.8 yuan interest. Vasin let Sanjay pay back 10 yuan because Sanjay was his relative and employee.

Ever since, Sanjay got stuck in the debts. In the fourth year, Sanjay had owed over 90 yuan to Vasin. In October that year, Sanjay didn't pay back his debts even with all his payments and grains on his own land.

Damayanti gave birth to their first child on the tenth day of the first lunar month, but her elder brother's wife was busy treating relatives in Spring Festival thus failing to take care of her. Sanjay could only cook rice soup for her.

As all grains had been given to Vasin, Sanjay's family had no food to eat during Spring Festival. Damayanti drunk rice soup made with a spoon of rice even she just had a baby. Sanjay was unwilling to drink his wife's soup or to cook meal with more rice, so he ate up Damayanti's leftover. The fact Sanjay only drank rice soup leftover for two days made Damayanti so heart-rending that she kept crying.

CHAPTER FOUR

On the 14th day of the first lunar year, the self-entertainment group planned a play to celebrate new year, so they came to invite Sanjay. At that time, Sanjay was too hungry to act in opera, so he refused and said: "I have to look after my newborn baby."

In daytime, others substituted Sanjay's part. However, audience were unsatisfied that Sanjay didn't appear in the opera till night. Some people yelled that: "Sanjay keeps up appearance even in our village. How dare him! No matter what reasons, we must see him today."

Hearing their words, the neighbor auntie replied hastily upstairs: "You don't know the actual situation. It is because they have no food. Sanjay didn't eat three or four days so he is weak now. How can he act in the opera?" Then, villagers all shouted: "Why not tell the truth earlier? We will send them some food. After all, it is Spring Festival." The neighbor auntie answered: "Sanjay was too shy to say such words. He was ashamed even I gave him a steamed bun." Vasin said: "Go to invite him again! The commune[3] will pay him and provide them food."

Sanjay was finally persuaded to act in the play for 3 days since he received money from the commune and steamed buns from the audience.

There was a custom in the village---audience should tip those people who act in the opera during Spring Festival.

Although it isn't a big money, no more than 20 cents, Sanjay got 30 cents since he was a good performer.

At that time, villagers would gamble for entertainment in the first lunar month. On the morning of 17th in the first lunar year, Sanjay who just got 30 cents from the temple, was stopped by a group of teenagers addicted to gambling. They forced Sanjay to gamble with them regardless of Sanjay's anxious expectation to go back home. Some thought Sanjay was hen-pecked, while others thought he cared too much about 30 cents. Their words were all mean, like "Does 30 cents equal to your life?" or "Sanjay wants to save the money for his own wife", which embarrassed Sanjay, so he decided to gamble with them. As a smart guy, he knew how to control himself. When he was still a boy, he would gamble with other children during Spring Festival but he gave up in recent years due to difficulties in life. For a while, Sanjay won over 1 yuan.

[1] mu, Chinese unit of land measurement that is commonly 666.7 square meters

[2] Long-term farm laborer work for landlord.

[3] It refers to people's commune, a kind of collective production system.

CHAPTER FIVE

Going back home, Damayanti told Sanjay, "The foreman came to find you. Vasin summoned his employees to work after the 15th day in the first lunar year." Sanjay answered: "I earn 1.5 yuan a month. I owed Vasin 90 yuan, so he earned 3.6 yuan from us per month under the condition that I work for him free of charge. I don't know how to cover the debts." Damayanti said, "If you don't work for him, how can we pay back the money?" Sanjay said, "I can find other jobs." "The money you earn from those jobs are all given to Vasin." Damayanti answered, "How can we live our own lives?". Sanjay yelled, "We have lost our own lives long ago."

Sanjay thought they would live in tough life whether he worked for Vasin or not. He made the decision to buy some rice first instead of working as land laborer. Then he shared the thought with Damayanti and went to the market with a bag.

When he passed a single man's home, Sanjay heard the noise of throwing coin[1] so he went into the house---it turned out to be those teenagers who gambled with him yesterday. A boy stopped him and shouted, "Why did you directly leave after winning money? It's unreasonable." Sanjay replied, "I wasn't responsible for your loss.", and wanted to leave. However, the teenage blocked him, patting coins in his pocket, and said, "You will win again if you are really capable."

Therefore, Sanjay gambled with them and didn't lose or win. A man came in and laid 1 yuan in the game. Most teenagers were too sacred to play with him (loser will lose a lot in the gamble), only leaving around 4 people. The teenage told Sanjay who wanted to leave that, "Your tricks only work on me. You must fail facing big man." Sanjay hated being regarded as inferior to others, so he gambled with that man and won 1 yuan. Then the man laid 2 yuan, and Sanjay followed despite that he thought it costed too much. Luckily, Sanjay won again, which irritated the man who laid 5 yuan then. This time, Sanjay lost. The veteran called him to work but Sanjay only replied, "I will think for a while. Maybe I won't work for Vasin." The teenager told the veteran that "It's critical moment. If he won, he could earn living expenses for months!" Without saying a word, the veteran left.

Soon, a child came in, shouted, "Run! The village head came to catch illegal gambling." The word shocked everyone, from gambler to observer, and they ran away immediately. Vasin didn't catch anyone finally.

At night when Sanjay returned home with rice, Vasin let the veteran to teach him a lesson and told him to continue to work. Sanjay proposed a requirement, "If you want me to work for you as long-term land laborer, you should lend me grains for a year firstly." Vasin thought to himself---Sanjay couldn't pay back debts even with all the harvests on his own land. How could he return other grains? It's more worthwhile hiring others---and then said, "OK. You don't have to work for me, but you must pay back 7 yuan interests last year now." Sanjay answered, "Take my 4 mu land! Even if I till land for a year, I still have to give the harvest to you."

It was settled. Two days later, Vasin asked his employees to till Sanjay's land.

It took Sanjay several years to ameliorate the land which was cultivated by others now. The fact annoyed Sanjay a lot, so he decided no longer went to the land. However, he lived closely to the land. Each time he went out, it would remind him that his land was occupied. Therefore, he stayed in the casino day after day. No matter he gambled or not, Sanjay was a regular visitor there. Gradually, Sanjay became indispensable for the casino too.

[1] It is a kind of gamble.

CHAPTER SIX

Ever since, Sanjay was addicted to gambling. At first, he only gambled within local casino, and then he was pulled to other villages. Sometimes, he would gamble outside for 3 months. The neighbor auntie told Damayanti that "You should persuade Sanjay not to gamble. If he really immerses in the abyss, he will ruin your life." Damayanti followed, but Sanjay said, "I don't care. I am a loser."

When he won some money, Sanjay would buy some food for Damayanti and their child; when he lost, he would rather to starve instead of coming back home. He knew gamble was wrong and didn't want his family to suffer. Damayanti understood Sanjay's idea so she followed him; she herself fed the family. She couldn't afford cotton when weaving cloth, so she worked for others to make money.

In winter, Damayanti got a piece of cloth as reward for her work when she was pregnant. She decided to use it to change rice. Sanjay came home, losing all money even his cotton-padded clothes. In freezing cold winter, Damayanti felt heart-broken seeing he was only in a crap suit.

On the 20th day in the first lunar month, Damayanti gave birth to their second child. Same as before, they had no rice left and their 4-year-old son cried due to empty stomach. So did Sanjay. Damayanti asked Sanjay to borrow rice from their neighbor and she would work for them to pay back. Sanjay did so. However, he was notorious as he was addicted to gamble so they rejected him. Hearing Damayanti and children's crying, their neighbor granny asked Sanjay, "I have an errand. Would you like to deal with my dead grandchild?" The first idea that struck Sanjay was "Why did you let me do such disgraceful thing? It's an insult." These words were not exported because he knew it was reasonable. "What's your opinion? Don't hesitate. It's better than borrow rice from others." The neighbor granny pressed. Sanjay agreed. He had lost his face long ago. He went out with a mat (wrapping the body). Sanjay chose byway in case of being noticed. Outside the village, he took a sneak at several person behind him. They were talking about him, but Sanjay didn't catch who they were and what they were talking about but his name. Under such circumstance, he had nowhere to hide himself or the mat, so he ran away as quickly as possible.

Sanjay earned 2-kilogram rice. Ever since, Sanjay seemed to be regarded as a practitioner. Any family losing children would pay Sanjay to deal with the body. Even teenagers in the village would tease that "If anyone of us died, we just need to contact Sanjay."

In the next Spring Festival, the self-entertainment group refused to act with Sanjay. They think it was shameful.

It seemed a truth: a person without self-respect will no longer care other's view or personal behavior. Sanjay became such a person. In summer, he would steal some food to fill the belly. If being caught, he would say nothing even being abused verbally or physically. For Sanjay, being full was more important than so-called "face".

In certain autumn, Vasin's relative told Vasin that Sanjay was caught in other village and fined 20 yuan because he stole carrots. Hearing the news, Damayanti went to seek help from Vasin. Actually, the reason Vasin's relative came here was to figure out whether Sanjay had any other belongings. If he had other possessions, Vasin could pay the fine firstly, and Vasin could require Sanjay to write an IOU; if not, he would send Sanjay into prison. Vasin thought although he plowed on Sanjay's 4 mu land, he hadn't got the title deed, and Sanjay still had two cottages. All Sanjay's belongings could cover 20-yuan fine, so Vasin decided to save Sanjay and said, "Damayanti, don't worry. I will deal with it." Finally, Sanjay was saved, but he wrote a contact to give his land and cottage to Vasin.

After getting land and cottage, Vasin, together with other relatives, came to teach Sanjay a lesson. At night, around 20 people caught Sanjay and bound him to a tree. Vasin gave orders to whip Sanjay with hemp rope no matter how Damayanti begged. Sanjay's skin split and flesh protruded, so he kept yelling.

It took a month for Sanjay to recover. During the period, they ran out of rice that Damayanti saved for over 6 months.

CHAPTER SEVEN

Damayanti hoped Sanjay stay at home but Sanjay refuted, "If I don't seek job outside, what can we eat?" Damayanti had no answer except weeping.

In winter, Sanjay went outside again. Less than a month later, he came back with new clothes and gave Damayanti 5 yuan, better than ever. Damayanti asked how could he earn the money, Sanjay only said "It's none of your business!" Damayanti bought some food and clothes for children with the money.

Villagers noticed Sanjay's children had new clothes and Damayanti didn't borrow rice, so they concluded that Sanjay must steal something expensive. Those who lost domestic animals or money all suspected him.

In the first lunar month, Vasin received a rich man's obituary, so he went to the town to offer his condolence. He found Sanjay was one of the two buglers who performed to see visitors out at the end of the funeral. Sanjay also saw him and then turned face.

Sanjay earned some money in the funeral. He thought he did nothing wrong, but Vasin didn't think so.

At night, Vasin summoned his relatives and told them, "Sanjay is such a bad guy. He works as bugler in the town and plays in the funeral. As a member of our family, he is losing our face. Others will misunderstand us! So disgraceful! We must find a solution." In the village, people emphasized family reputation and regarded "bugler" as shame. Therefore, they were mad at Sanjay after hearing Vasin's words and some of them even shouted "Kill him!" or "Bury him!". The neighbor auntie heard the news and told Damayanti. Sanjay ran away immediately.

Damayanti hadn't heard from Sanjay over 7 years since then. She lived with their two children. The elderly one was 15 years old, working as a cowherd. Other children often cursed at him.

One year after Sanjay left, Japanese invaded the village. Some people persuaded Damayanti, "Why not marry others? It's meaningless to waste your life for a bad guy. There are a lot of good men in the world." Damayanti refused and said, "You don't know the real situation. Sanjay isn't bad."

Hearing Sanjay's story, village cadre and director went to talk with him. The director said, "We have punished Vasin and returned all the things he forcibly occupied. You are victim so we decide to give you land and you can feed on it. Do you agree?" Sanjay yelled, "I don't care about that. What I need is a public apology from Vasin! It's unfair to be misunderstood for so many years." Village cadre and director promised him.

At night, villagers gathered to have a meeting, and Sanjay also participated. The village director pointed out the aim of the meeting but some people were unwilling to have any contact with Sanjay. No matter what others feel, Sanjay said, "I have been back for half a month, but no one wants to connect with me because you thought me as a bad guy. However, tonight, I want to debate about what I have done with the honorable family member---Vasin, and I hope you serve as the judge. Don't worry. It's a new society." Then he turned to Vasin, "Mr. Vista, you have to spare more energy and time on jerk like me. Our debt is clear: I owed you 30 yuan and around 60 kilograms rice. You took 3 cottages, 4 mu land from me and I worked for you 5 years without wages. I don't want to bother about that now. I just want you to judge whether I am a good man or not!"

Looking around without a word for a while, Vasin said, "If you have resentful feelings towards me, you can just tell directly. I have compensated all I got illegally and you are the last one. You can't bully me. I still have a big shop!"

Fugue said, "I am not here to bully you, Mr.Vista. I don't want compensation. I just need you to tell everyone I am not a jerk! I did nothing bad until I was 18 years old." Others echoed Sanjay "Yes. Tell the truth." Sanjay continued, "Later, I started to gamble, steal and became a jerk eventually. I have done many wrong things and I don't blame anyone. I have reflected on my mistakes. I am not a good people according to your principle. You want me to work for you and to occupy my land. At the end of each year, my wages and harvest from the land are all used to pay back interests, leaving no food for my family. It's a vicious circle! Why do I gamble? Why do I steal things? Why do I become a jerk? It's because I'm hungry and I have no food. In order to hold my mother's funeral, I bought a coffin and other things from your shop and I'm afraid I can't pay back so I work for you for 5 years. Even so, I lost my land finally so had no harvest. It has been 6 years since I caught bad habits. During the period, I have been abused, beaten, crying and starving numerous times. Villagers still call me jerk this year and curse my son. It's all because of you! To prevent from being punished, I went to Liao county in which I still gamble and steal to feed myself. Later, Japanese came so no one had time to tease me. Then I was educated by new government, and I went to till new land in the mountain. Since then, I had my own land, cottage and food again, but I still did not dare to come back to look after my wife and children. Over the past 7 years outside, I bought a cow, accumulated rice and other food there. I have had been aimed to take over my family and have no plan to get even with you. However, people in the village were unwilling to talk to me, maybe being afraid of being stolen or thinking me as jerk. I don't want to leave under a notorious cap. Mr.Vista, please tell everyone whether I am a jerk or not! Who should be responsible for all my difficulties?"

9 798889 594383

Printed by Libri Plureos GmbH in Hamburg,
Germany